LITTLE LIBRARY

Guide to
Germany

Madeline McHugh & Birgit Balzert

Kingfisher Books

NEW YORK

Contents

Welcome to Germany

The tour bus pulls up in the sleepy square of a southern village. All around, high mountains look down on a cluster of neat wooden houses, each built with a steep roof to protect against winter snows. But this is only one small corner of a big country. There's far more yet to explore — as you'll soon see.

The heart of Europe

Germany lies right in the very middle of Europe. To the south it rises into the Alps. Two great rivers cross this part of the country — the Danube and the Rhine. Berlin, the capital, is in the northeast of Germany. The far north has a bustling harbor at Hamburg, as well as rolling dunes and sandy beaches all along the coastlines of the North and Baltic seas.

GERMAN MONEY

In Germany, the money people use is called marks and pfennigs. When you go to a bank, you'll see signs showing how much German money you can get in exchange for your own money.

NORTH SEA

BALTIC SEA

Denmark

Kiel

Hamburg

R. Weser

R. Elbe

Bremen

Hanover

Berlin

R. Rhine

Dresden

Frankfurt

Czech Republic

GERMANY

France

Black Forest

R. Danube

ALPS

ALPS

Munich

Switzerland

Austria

7

In a German town

The buildings in many German towns are hundreds of years old. At the heart of most towns is a main square with a clock tower. Here, there may also be a few market stalls or stands selling hot snacks. Often, there are also outdoor cafés where people stop for coffee or a glass of beer.

①

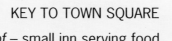

KEY TO TOWN SQUARE

1. *Gasthof* – small inn serving food
2. *Kirche* – town church or cathedral
3. *Bäckerei* – bakery selling bread and rolls
4. *Spielwarengeschäft* – toy store
5. *Zeitungsstand* – newsdealer
6. *Postamt* – post office

Going shopping

German shops open early, usually at 8 or 9 A.M., and stay open to 6 P.M. They close about midday on Saturdays.

Toy stores are wonderful places to visit. They stock hundreds of brightly painted toy trains, cars, planes, and even model castles and villages that are perfect in every detail. Many shops also sell small cuckoo clocks that you can put together yourself.

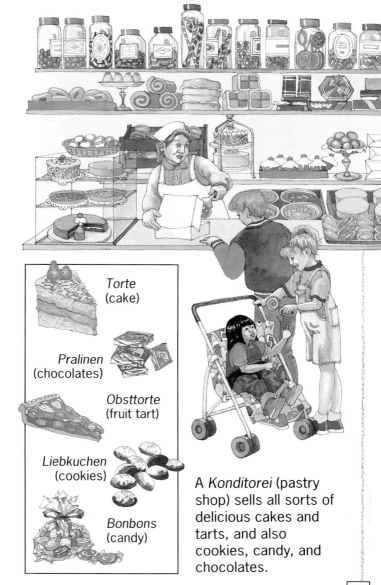

Torte
(cake)

Pralinen
(chocolates)

Obsttorte
(fruit tart)

Liebkuchen
(cookies)

Bonbons
(candy)

A *Konditorei* (pastry shop) sells all sorts of delicious cakes and tarts, and also cookies, candy, and chocolates.

11

Eating and drinking

Two things Germany is famous for are *sauerkraut* (pickled cabbage) and beer. But there are also dozens of breads, from crusty white to dark rye, and more kinds of sausage than days in the year. Many dishes are named after their region — frankfurters are from Frankfurt, and *Schwarzwaldtorte* is a delicious cherry and chocolate cake from the Black Forest.

Pretzels are salty snacks, nibbled with a tankard of refreshing ice-cold beer.

Kartoffelpuffer are fried potato cakes, often eaten with homemade apple sauce.

KARTOFFELPUFFER

Ask a grown-up to help you cook these potato cakes. You'll need:

1 lb potatoes
½ onion
1 egg
2 tbsp. flour
1 tsp. salt

1 Peel and grate the potatoes and finely chop the onion. Mix in the salt, egg, and flour.
2 Put a spoonful of the mixture into hot oil, flatten it into a pancake, and fry it until golden brown on both sides.

13

Things to see and do

The northern town of Hamelin is famous for its Pied Piper. The story goes that the Piper was asked to clear the town of rats, but when he wasn't paid he led the children away with his enchanted flute. Today the story is remembered with a festival — there are even little rat candies to nibble on!

Every Sunday during the summer, an actor dresses up as the Piper and tootles his flute in Hamelin town square.

Children dressed in rat costumes follow after him. The action all takes place on a stage outside the town hall.

The eastern town of Meissen is where porcelain was first made in Europe. You can visit the factory to watch china being handpainted.

PAINT YOUR OWN CHINA

Here's how to turn a plain china plate into a stunning creation of your own. You'll need a white china plate, a grease pencil, and ceramic paints (from an art store), as well as paintbrushes and mineral spirits.

1 Draw the pattern or picture you want on paper first, then copy it onto the plate with the pencil.
2 Paint your pattern, then leave it to dry. (Clean off the brushes in mineral spirits after you finish.)

The Black Forest

This region of wild woods and valleys in southwest Germany is where many people go on walking vacations in summer and cross-country skiing in winter. The area is also famous for its cuckoo clocks. If you go to the town of Furtwangen, you can visit a museum with one of the most amazing clock collections in the world.

Wild boar and deer make their homes in some of the quieter corners of the Black Forest region.

Castle country

Princes and robber barons who lived along the Rhine valley often built castles on rocky hilltops, from which they plundered the surrounding country. Today many of these castles are in ruins, although some are still open to visitors.

Neuschwanstein is a castle built in Bavaria just over 100 years ago. Walt Disney used it as a model for the castle in his film *The Sleeping Beauty*.

Two great cities

G ermany has many great cities, but two that most visitors try to see are Berlin, the capital, and Munich.

The heart of Munich is the square called Marienplatz. On one side is a large town hall and clock tower.

As the Marienplatz clock strikes, its statues of dancers, musicians, and jousting knights perform.

The Brandenburg Gate is a great landmark in the middle of Berlin. It was built by a German king over 200 years ago.

CHARLOTTENBURG PALACE

A high clock tower rises over this vast palace built in Berlin in the late 1600s. The rooms are richly decorated, and nowadays you can visit the magnificent royal apartments where the kings and queens of Germany once lived.

19

Traveling around

Germany is crisscrossed by busy highways and ultrafast express trains. In crowded cities, underground trains or trams are often used to get around the heavy traffic. Out in the countryside, good roads make it easy to drive just about anywhere.

Special mountain trains run up into the Alps in the south of the country. They can climb steep tracks and cope with deep snowdrifts.

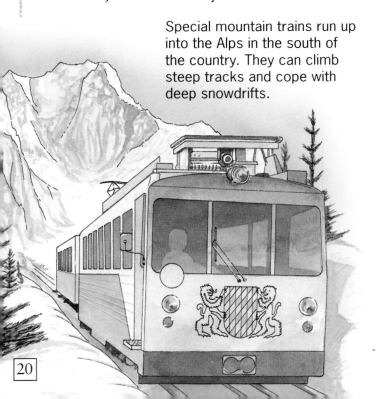

△ Electric trams run in big cities. They run on special tracks where other traffic can't go.

▽ A German highway is called an *Autobahn*. Though wide, roads can be choked with traffic.

Sports and games

The three great sports in Germany are skiing, tennis, and soccer. The Germans are enthusiastic supporters of their national soccer team, which has won the World Cup several times.

Many schools teach soccer, tennis, and swimming in the afternoon. During vacations, the entire class may go to the mountains to walk or ski — downhill and cross-country are popular.

World champions like Boris Becker, Michael Stich, and Steffi Graf have made tennis a craze in Germany. There are courts almost everywhere, full of people hard at work practicing to be future stars!

Hang gliding and paragliding are popular sports in hilly country. Both make use of rising winds to soar and glide over the land.

There are enough footpaths in Germany to go around the world three times. People can be found taking long walks in forests and mountains at any time of the year.

23

School and play

School starts early in Germany. By 8 A.M., students are all sitting in class. Soon after 1 P.M., school finishes and everyone goes home for a big lunch. In the afternoon, students do homework, or return to school for sports or music lessons.

On the day they first start school, at six years old, children are given a big paper cone stuffed with candy and little toys as a treat.

Many people go to the
seashore in summer.
The wind is strong on
the North Sea coast, so
people rent beach
chairs to sunbathe
in comfort.

PLAY RINGBALL

Mark out a big ring, about 25 feet wide, on
the ground. Set a box in the middle, with one
player to guard it. Everyone else forms a ring
around the box.

The ring players have to hit the box by
throwing a ball, while the player in the middle
keeps the ball away. Whoever hits the box is
next in the middle.

Celebrations

German children are lucky. They have two chances to get presents at Christmas. The night before December 6th, Saint Nicholas fills the shoes of good children with gifts of fruit, nuts, and small toys.

A few days later, on Christmas Eve itself, everybody finds piles of presents under the Christmas tree.

In October, a great beer festival is held in Munich, bringing thousands of people into the city. Many dress in the traditional clothes of the region, which is known as Bavaria.

EASTER EGGS

In Germany, the Easter Bunny hides brightly colored eggs in the yard for children to find! You can decorate Easter eggs too. All you need is:

White eggs
Onion skins
   (for yellow)
Beets (red)
Spinach (green)
Poster paints

1 Dye an egg by hardboiling it with a vegetable.
2 As soon as the egg cools, you can paint it.

Christmas trees in German homes are always decorated with candles — either real or electric ones. Lots of pretty decorations and sometimes even small chocolates are hung on the boughs.

Let's speak German!

NUMBERS

1	eins
2	zwei
3	drei
4	vier
5	fünf
6	sechs
7	sieben
8	acht
9	neun
10	zehn

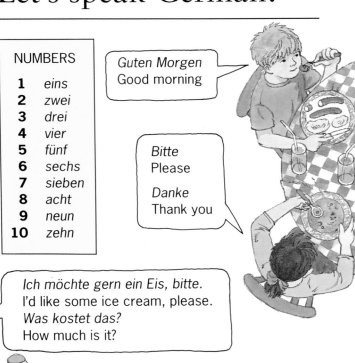

Guten Morgen
Good morning

Bitte
Please

Danke
Thank you

Ich möchte gern ein Eis, bitte.
I'd like some ice cream, please.
Was kostet das?
How much is it?

Sprichst du Englisch?
Do you speak English?

Nein
No

Ja
Yes

Index